SUN UP, SUN DOWN

THE STORY OF DAY AND NIGHT

OH, GOOD... A BEDTIME STORY.

Jacqui Bailey Matthew Lilly

A & C BLACK • LONDON

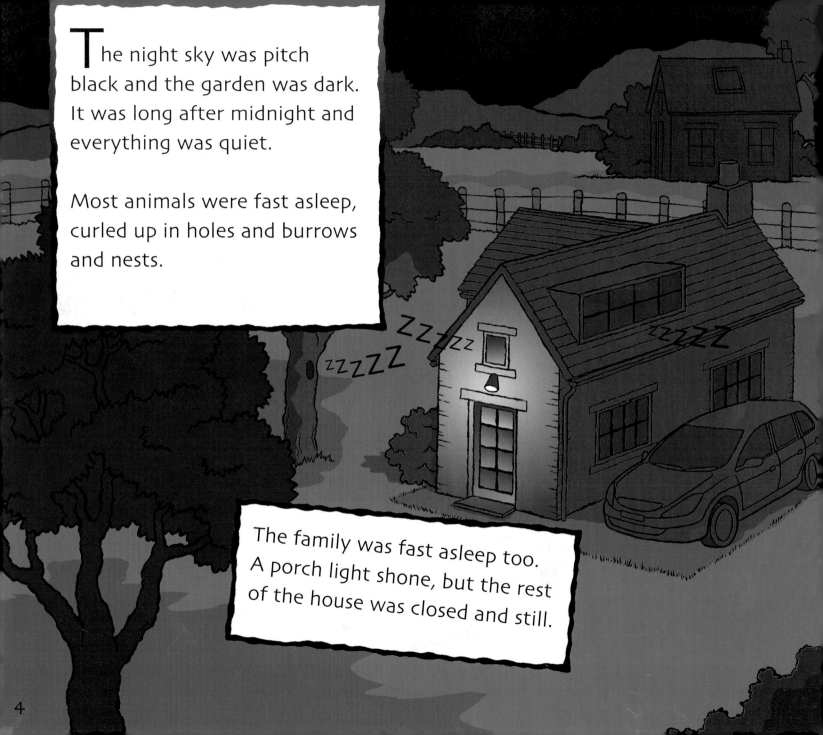

The night sky was pitch black and the garden was dark. It was long after midnight and everything was quiet.

Most animals were fast asleep, curled up in holes and burrows and nests.

The family was fast asleep too. A porch light shone, but the rest of the house was closed and still.

Then a breeze rustled the leaves of a tree. Behind the house, a strip of light appeared between the land and the sky.

The light grew stronger and brighter. It pushed back the dark and the sky changed from black to grey to blue.

Streaks of sunlight raced over the land and the Sun bulged into view.

It was dawn — time to start another day.

Bit by bit the Sun rose in the sky, sending out its beams of light, called rays.

When the rays hit the garden they started warming everything up.

The damp grass steamed as it began to dry — and life suddenly got busier.

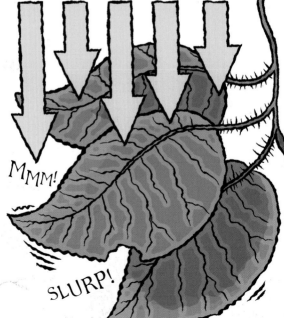

MMM!

SLURP!

Plants lifted up their leaves and greedily soaked up the Sun's rays. It had been a long, dark night and they needed the energy in the sunlight to make their food.

Insects uncurled and crawled into the sunshine. Other animals stretched and yawned. They were hungry too.

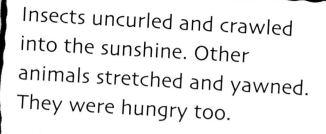

OOOH, THAT'S BETTER. NOTHING LIKE A BIT OF SUNLIGHT TO START THE DAY.

MMM, BREAKFAST!

MMM, BREAKFAST!

Some chomped on plants . . . some gobbled up insects . . .

MMM, BREAKFAST!

. . . and some ate just about anything they could get their hands on!

But imagine what would happen if the Sun didn't rise . . .

I NEED SUN!

Without its light and warmth all the plants on Earth would starve and die.

I NEED GREENS!

If the plants died, then the plant-eating animals would die, too.

And if the plant-eating animals died, there would be nothing for the other animals to eat, either.

I NEED MEAT!

Earth would be dark and cold and empty. It's lucky for us we have the Sun!

The Sun's light and heat shine so strongly on us, you might think it was close by. But it's not. It's millions and millions of kilometres away.

The reason we can see and feel it from so far away is because the Sun itself is incredibly bright and hot. So hot, that it's impossible to get anywhere near it. Scientists can take photographs of it, though . . .

RUMBLE!
RUMBLE!
BOOM!
BOOM!

RUMBLE!
RUMBLE!
BOOM!

. . . and they've discovered that the Sun is a gigantic ball of superhot gases. Deep inside it, billions of explosions are taking place every second, and it is these explosions that create all that raging heat and light.

The Sun was giving out other types of rays, too!

Some of the Sun's other rays, such as x-rays and ultraviolet rays, can be harmful to life on Earth.

Luckily, many of them are blocked out by Earth's atmosphere — this is the band of gases that covers the Earth — but some do get through.

So the children covered themselves in sun lotion to help block out any harmful rays that might damage their skin.

With the Sun high overhead, it was hard to find anywhere shady and cool in the garden.

The children put up a big umbrella and sat in the shadow beneath it.

Light rays can pass through some materials — the same ones you can see through, such as glass and clear plastic.

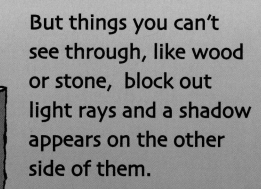

But things you can't see through, like wood or stone, block out light rays and a shadow appears on the other side of them.

All kinds of things make shadows on sunny days — houses, trees, fences, flower pots, even you! But shadows are always changing.

1 In the morning, when the Sun is low down in the sky, the shadows are long.

2 As the Sun climbs higher, the shadows get shorter.

3 When the Sun is at its highest, there are almost no shadows at all.

4 In the afternoon, the shadows get longer again — but this time they are on the other side!

The garden sweltered in the afternoon heat. But the Sun didn't stay high overhead.

It gradually swung across to the other side of the sky and slid towards the land.

IS IT SUPPER TIME YET?

Slowly the shadows lengthened and the sky grew darker.

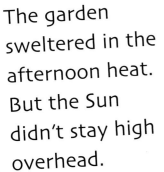

EEEEK!

I PREFER FOOD FROM A TIN.

Most of the animals in the garden (and the family) got ready to go to sleep. But not all! Some liked the dark and coolness of evening — for them it was the best time to find their food.

The Sun sank into the ground and the last bits of sunlight glowed orange and red in the sky. Then the Sun was gone. The sky was black and it was night time again.

But, hang on a minute, the Sun hadn't really gone into the ground . . . had it?

Well, no, it hadn't. It hadn't moved across the sky at all. It just looked like it had. In fact, it was the Earth that moved — but you'd have to be in a spaceship to see it!

From a spaceship you would see the Earth as a bright, beautiful ball, hanging in the blackness of Space.

But it's not just hanging there – it's moving all the time. It's spinning around and around, just like a giant spinning top.

As the Earth spins, half of it is turned away from the Sun. The Sun's light doesn't reach it so for this side it's night time...

ZZZZZZ

The spinning doesn't make us dizzy because the Earth never ever changes its speed or the direction in which it spins. And we're so used to it, we don't feel a thing!

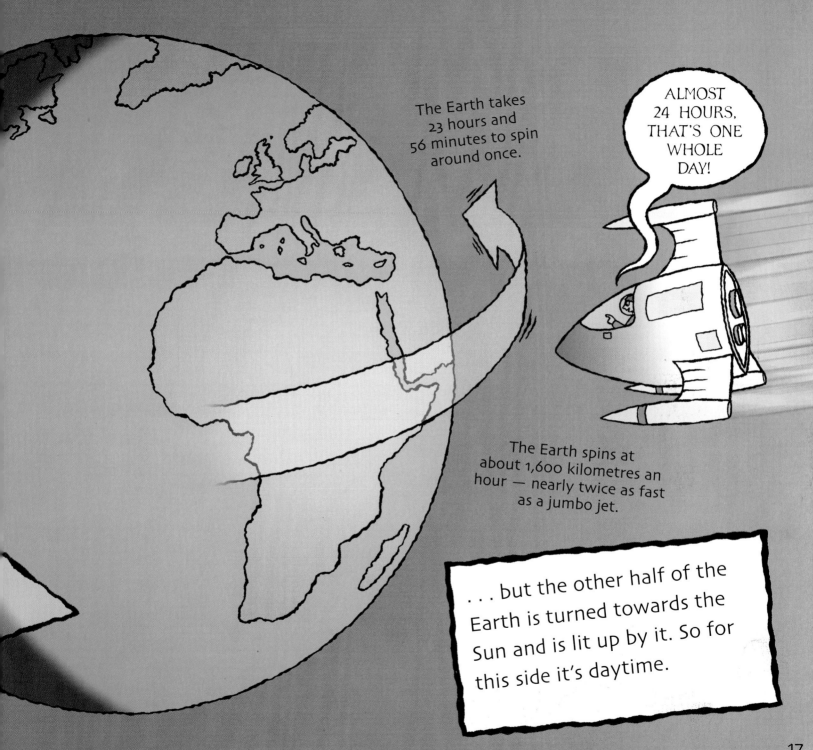

The Earth takes 23 hours and 56 minutes to spin around once.

ALMOST 24 HOURS, THAT'S ONE WHOLE DAY!

The Earth spins at about 1,600 kilometres an hour — nearly twice as fast as a jumbo jet.

. . . but the other half of the Earth is turned towards the Sun and is lit up by it. So for this side it's daytime.

1 At dawn, when the Sun rose over the garden, this part of the Earth was just turning towards the Sun.

2 At midday, the garden was face to face with the Sun.

3 When it was evening in the garden, this part of the Earth was turning away from the Sun.

4 At midnight, the garden was facing the opposite direction to the Sun. It was in the Earth's shadow.

However . . . even though it was night time in the garden, the sky wasn't entirely black. A glowing lantern of light hung there. It was the Moon.

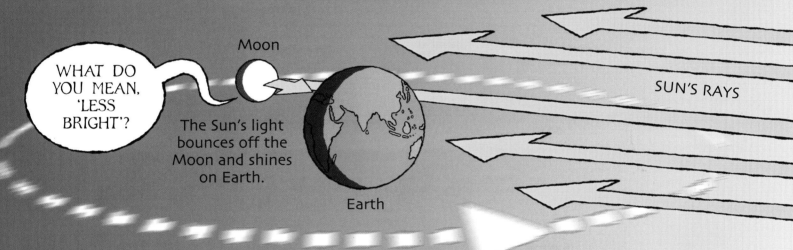

WHAT DO YOU MEAN, 'LESS BRIGHT'?

Moon

The Sun's light bounces off the Moon and shines on Earth.

Earth

SUN'S RAYS

The Moon is far less bright than the Sun. That's because it doesn't make any light of its own. It is a lifeless ball of rock. It only shines because the Sun's light is bouncing off it.

The Moon is our closest neighbour in Space, but it isn't only a neighbour. It travels around and around the Earth — just as the Earth travels around the Sun.

That's right! The Earth moves in two completely different ways. As well as spinning around on itself, it's also travelling in circles (well, sort of egg-shaped circles) around the Sun! This huge, looping journey is called an orbit.

It takes the Earth 365.25 days to make one complete orbit of the Sun. That's one whole year.

DON'T YOU GUYS EVER GET TIRED OF DOING THE SAME OLD THING?

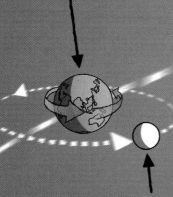

The Moon orbits the Earth while the Earth orbits the Sun.

Earth's orbit is 958 million kilometres long, and the Earth zips around it at 108,000 kilometres per hour — that's almost four times the speed of a Space Shuttle!

The Earth never stops, or slows down. It's been orbiting the Sun for about 4 ½ billion years, and it will keep going for billions more.

And do you know what the really amazing thing is?
Earth's orbit is exactly the right distance from the Sun!

HURRAY!

HURRAY!

Any closer, and the Earth would get too hot. The oceans would dry up and the world would be an empty desert.

Any further away and the Earth would get too cold. The whole world would become a huge iceball.

But the Earth is not too close, or too far away. So we have just the right amount of heat and light for plants and animals — including us — to live.

And that's nearly the end of the story . . . but not quite . . . because the Moon wasn't the only light in the night sky. There were also hundreds, even thousands of tiny twinkling pinpricks of light. They were stars!

WOW! LOOK AT ALL THOSE STARS. . .

But even the stars aren't really the way they look from Earth.

Those tiny twinkling lights are billions upon billions of kilometres away, and every single one of them is a gigantic, glowing, scorchingly hot sun, like our own.

WHICH IS BIGGEST?

From Earth, the Sun and the Moon look much the same size. But the Moon is really only a quarter of the size of Earth, whereas the Sun is more than a hundred times bigger!

So if the Earth was the size of a cherry stone, then the Sun would be as big as a beachball, and the Moon would be almost as small as a pinhead!

I'M SCARED!

HOW FAR?

ZOOOMMM!

PUFF! PANT!

The Sun is 150 million kilometres from Earth. If you climbed in a car and drove there at 100 kilometres per hour, it would take you about 171 years to arrive. Although the heat from the Sun would have fried you to a crisp long before you got there!

But sunlight travels much faster. It takes just over 8 minutes for a ray of sunlight to get from the Sun to the surface of the Earth.

MOVING AROUND

No matter where you live on Earth, the Sun always rises more or less in the east and sets more or less in the west.

Exactly where you see the Sun rise or set depends on what time of year it is. In winter the Sun is lower in the sky than in summer, even at midday. And it rises later and sets earlier.

Midday is the half-way point between rising and setting, when the Sun is at its highest in the sky. We say that midday is at 12 o'clock, but the Sun doesn't always reach its highest point at exactly this time.

Midday
in summer

Midday
in winter

Sunrise

Sunset

GIANTS AND DWARFS

Even stars don't last forever. One day, about 5 billion years from now, our Sun will start to go out.

To begin with it will swell up — growing as much as 100 times bigger. It will become what scientists call a 'red giant'. Hopefully, by this time we'll have moved somewhere else, as Earth will be baked to a cinder.

Then the Sun will start to shrink. Over millions more years it will turn into a small white star about the size of Earth. Scientists call this a 'white dwarf'. After this, our Sun will slowly fade away.

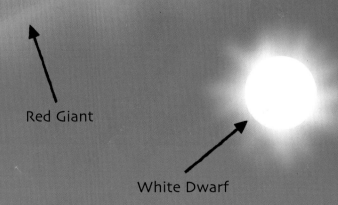

Red Giant

White Dwarf

TRY IT AND SEE

SUN TIME

Thousands of years ago, before we invented clocks and watches, people used the Sun to help them measure time. They did it by making something called a sundial.

OH GOOD, IT'S TIME FOR TEA.

Have a go at making your own sundial. It will take the best part of a day, so choose a time when you don't have to be anywhere special — and when the Sun is shining!

You will need:
- A large sheet of white card or paper
- Some plasticine or play dough
- A wooden stick, such as a pencil
- A felt-tip pen and a ruler
- An alarm clock

1 Choose a good spot to make your sundial. It needs to be outside in the open where no shadows will fall on it as the day goes by — and where it won't be moved.

2

Put the sheet of paper or card on a firm, flat surface — such as a table, a paving stone, or even an upturned tray or cardboard box.

If you are using paper, put a stone on each corner to hold the paper in place.

3 Use the plasticine to make a base for the wooden stick. Make sure the stick will stand upright. Then place the stick and the base in the middle of your paper. Draw a circle around the base to mark its position and don't move it.

The stick is called the gnomon (*no-mon*). When the Sun shines on it, the gnomon will make a shadow on the paper.

4 Start as early as you can in the morning. Set your alarm clock to go off every hour during the day so you don't forget. Each time the alarm goes off, check the position of the shadow on the paper and draw a line along it with the felt-tip and ruler.

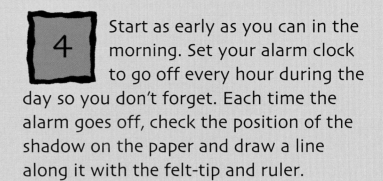

Keep your sundial in place and the next day you can use it to find out what the time is without looking at a clock. As long as the Sun is shining, of course!

SHINING FACTS

The Sun's light may only take about 8 minutes to get to the Earth, but the energy that creates it takes over a million years to get from the centre of the Sun to its surface.

BRIGHT... YET VERY SLOW.

THIS COULD TAKE SOME TIME.

The distance from one star to another is so vast that scientists measure distance in 'light-years'. One light-year is the distance travelled by a light ray in one year — which is 9,500 billion kilometres!

The surface of the Sun seems smooth from a distance, but it is always bubbling with energy. Every now and then, huge flares of hot gas spurt out into Space. They can stretch for thousands of kilometres before falling back to the Sun.

INDEX

SOME SUNNY WEBSITES TO VISIT

http://amazing-space.stsci.edu = Amazing Space: Education On-Line from the Hubble Space Telescope. A brilliant site with loads of activities all about Space.

http://starchild.gsfc.nasa.gov = StarChild: 'A Learning Center for Young Astronomers', created by NASA's High Energy Astrophysics Science Archive Research Center, which is a very complicated name for such a fun site!

http://observe.arc.nasa.gov = NASA's Observatorium. Go to the 'Gallery' for fabulous photos of views of the Earth and Space.

For Vickie
JB

For Oliver, Timothy and Gregory
ML

First published in 2003 by
A & C Black Publishers Limited
37 Soho Square, London W1D 3QZ
www.acblack.com

Created for A & C Black Publishers Limited by
two's COMPANY
Copyright © Two's Company 2003

The rights of Jacqui Bailey and Matthew Lilly
to be identified as the author and the illustrator of this
work have been asserted by them in accordance with
the Copyrights, Designs and Patents Act 1988.

ISBN 0 7136 6253 0 (hbk)
ISBN 0 7136 6254 9 (pbk)

Printed in Hong Kong by Wing King Tong

A & C Black uses paper produced with elemental chlorine-free
pulp, harvested from managed sustainable forests.